Life in a
Crazy California Condo

An Adult Literacy and
English Language Learning Novelette

By Glorious Fealing

© Glorious Fealing 2021
Life in a Crazy California Condo
Suggested Intermediate Level

ISBN: 9781736848005

1

Author's Note

This book is dedicated to my students. My students have expressed the desire to build reading fluency. This book will help with reading fluency because it offers a simple plot using simple language, making it potentially quick and easy to read.

I wrote this book because my students wanted to read books more suitable to their position as adults learning English as an additional language or generally learning to read English to build literacy skills. They needed easy-to-read books with themes that adults could relate to. However, we were only able to find children's books at the desired reading level. This book serves the purpose of providing easy reading with themes that potentially interest adult readers.

How to Get the Most Out of This Book

As you read this book, you should also use a dictionary or translation technology such as an app on your cell phone.

Make sure you understand all of the words as you read. Use a vocabulary notebook. Write new words and definitions and translations in your vocabulary notebook. This will show you how many new words you have learned while reading this book and could potentially help you to learn English faster.

The Purpose of
This Book

This book is like a shorter version of a novel. The person who reads this book will prepare to read longer, more complex works while enjoying the satisfaction of having finished reading a novelette. It intends to be a gateway to reading longer works and it seeks to encourage students to read more challenging books as their desire to read grows.

For more information about my other publications or to take a class with me, visit my website:
https://sites.google.com/view/gfUSAEnglish.

Foreword by Laura Trent

Tap tap! Knock knock!

Who can it be?

Glorious Fealing brings us to a simple reading and storytelling of a crazy condo experience. Is it a thriller or just mysterious happenings on a new life journey where the unexpected becomes reality?

Glorious' simplicity and targeted writing will help people understand and enjoy reading. It will help all of those who are learning English with curiosity and willingness to reach the end of this beautiful novelette.

Foreword by
Laura Migliorini

I read this story in two different days. I wanted to leave room for my curiosity without discovering everything immediately. I managed to understand despite my lack of English and to feel the anxiety that a good thriller can give you, thanks to the simplicity of Glorious' writing, who knows perfectly well how to make something simple that might not always be simple.

Foreword by
Mukadder Kocabiyik

The author of the book is my **"Glorious"** teacher. I have a long friendship with her and she is my role model. *"Life in a Crazy California Condo"* is helping students improve the reading, listening, and pronunciation skills.

The book is a very fruitful book for adult English learners, no matter your current skill level. Because the author chooses the story from real life, the reader can be more interested in the story.

I like the vocabulary chosen because it is very simple with easy pronunciation. The writer uses short and emotional sentences in this book. I think the use of this is an important detail.

Author Glorious Fealing writes in a clear, easily accessible style, addressing English learners and readers. Thank you, thank you, thank you for this book.

I am excited to recommend this book, my friend.

"Have fun –"

Table of Contents

Life in a
Crazy California Condo

Blue skies, ocean waves, and warm ocean air. I breathed deeply and took it all in.

Could there be a more perfect day?

I had fallen asleep at the beach and slept surprisingly well in the driver's seat. I pulled back into traffic and drove back to my condo.

The place was beautiful. Hardwood floors. Floor to ceiling mirrors. Brand new kitchen and bathroom tile work. It was a dream come true. . . until the craziness started.

I sat down to eat dinner and turned on the T.V.

Tap-tap-tap.

I turned around to see if someone were at the window. No one was there.

I went back to dinner and my show.

Tap-tap-tap. It was louder this time.

I hit mute and checked my kitchen sink. The water was off. I checked under the sink.

1

Nothing. Cabinets. Nothing. Bathroom. Nothing. I checked the balcony. Nothing.

I went back to my show.

Strange.

I tried to eat. I watched my show on mute just to see if the tapping would start again. If I had mice in this beautiful condo, I would be really angry. It was my first night in here. I had just bought the place.

Please don't let it be ruined on the first night!

I continued eating in silence. By now my show was off so I decided to catch up on some work. I turned on the computer and worked well into the night. I was still excited about this new condo and I was not going to let some tapping bring me down from my high.

The next morning, I was awakened by classical piano. I got out of bed wondering where the music was coming from. Across the quad, I saw my neighbor's son banging away.

Sunday at 9:00 a.m.

I looked at my watch and noted the time and day.

I guess I am going to have to go back to the beach if I want to sleep in.

The music was nice until he hit a sour note. On and on he practiced.

Boy am I glad I don't live upstairs from him.

I came home from work the next day. I kicked off my shoes and stretched out on the floor.

"I love you, condo." I told it. The walls seemed to love me back. The ceiling smiled down on me.

My cell phone rang.

"Hey, Vic'." I said.

"Hey! How's life in your new condo?" She asked.

"Great." I answered.

"I know it is everything you wanted."

"For sure. How are your husband and the kids?"

"They're all just fine. Well, this was just a quick 'thinking of you' call to see how you were settling in. I'll catch you later."

"Okay.

I lay there, loving my condo. I waited for more tapping. So far, nothing.

A week had passed in my condo. There was no more tapping.

3

I came home from work a little later than usual. I kicked off my shoes and lay on the floor.

"I love you, condo." I told it. I closed my eyes. The floor reached up and hugged me. The walls reached around and hugged me. The ceiling smiled at me again.

Knock-knock-knock.

"You've got to be kidding me." I said softly.

I did not answer the door. I waited.

Knock-knock-knock.

I sat in the silence.

They kept knocking for a few minutes and then finally gave up.

All of my friends know to call or text me first. Do not just show up at my door. So, the person, whoever it was, was a stranger.

A few more days passed. I came home from work. As I walked toward the door, I saw a note on the door post. Uneasiness washed over me as I grabbed the note.

You have the weirdest "stuff" going on down there.

Have no idea why you run so much water.

Also, that 'noise' from that electrical tool you had going all night kept me AWAKE! DISTURBING THE PEACE!!

Police will be out to investigate you –

Weird stuff with that cart too!

Yeah, you sell insurance out of Solana Beach. Sure – what a lie – even Lilly tried to tell me that.

Have fun –

I was in panic mode. I rushed into the house, double locked the door, and called my parents.

"Mom. Dad. Are you both on?" I asked.

"What's the matter, Jill?" My mom asked, alarmed. I am sure she heard the panic in my voice.

"I don't know what's going on." I told them.

"Baby girl, what is it?" My father asked.

I told them all about the note and the knocking and the tapping.

"That's got to be a mistake." My mom said.

"Yes. They probably put it on the wrong door." My dad said.

"You guys think so?" I asked.

"Yes." My dad said. "Keep it handy anyway. Start taking notes about the things that concern you, just in case."

"Okay." My dad always had good advice. My parents always knew how to help me calm down.

I was still shaken. My perfect condo seemed to love me, but I was having a strange introduction to the place. I took my parents' advice. I fixed myself some tea and stretched out on the floor again.

Try to relax.

The next day, I came home from work. I approached my door. There was no note. That was a relief.

I kicked off my shoes and sat down to eat dinner.

I breathed in and out deeply.

Knock-knock-knock.

"Not again." I said softly.

My cell phone rang.

"Victoria, oh, my goodness." I said.

"Girl, what?" She asked.

"Every few days someone's been knocking on my door. It's been weird since I moved in. I don't talk to anyone and I keep to myself. I like it that way." I told her.

The knocking got louder.

"You'd think people would get the message if I don't answer." I said.

I drew my breath in suddenly.

"What, Jill? Talk to me." She said.

"The person held up an envelope to the window and asked if it was my mail." I told her.

"What?" She said.

"Yeah. If you got the wrong mail, just put it back into the mailbox to return to sender." I said softly.

"Is this your mail?" The voice outside got louder.

"Wow! Even I heard it this time." Victoria was amazed.

"Girl, yeah. I know they can hear me walking and talking. Do they really think I am going to open that door?" I was in slight disbelief.

"Do you have anything you can use to protect yourself in case you get attacked?" Victoria asked me.

"My pretty face?" I asked. "Do you think that will save me?"

"How about a kitchen knife?" She asked.

"I could, but I am not that strong, so they might take the knife and use it on me." I said.

"Frick." She said.

Victoria stayed on the phone with me until the person finally gave up and walked away. We talked for a few hours until I calmed down.

"Girl, this place was so perfect at first, but now it's starting to be a real pain."

"Well, at least they went away." She said.

"Yeah. For now." I said.

"I am worried about you there all alone." She said.

"That makes two of us." I said. "But I can't live in fear. Let me sleep on it and decide what I can do in the morning."

"Please call me tomorrow. I'll be thinking about this all night." She said.

"Will do." I promised.

I could not sleep that night. I woke up around 4:00 a.m. and wrote down all of the weird things that happened to me like the tapping, the note, the two visits from the strangers. I wrote down the dates and times. I started getting sleepy around 7:00 a.m. My body was merciful and let me sleep for a couple of hours. I was interrupted by a knock on the door. I woke up annoyed. It was Saturday, so I knew I could get a nap later. The person knocked louder and louder.

It was morning this time, so I felt like I could answer the door.

"Hello." I said.

There stood a middle-aged brunette lady with a not-so-friendly face.

"I am having trouble with my water. Are you having trouble with your water?" She asked.

"No." I answered.

"I am having trouble flushing the toilet and there's no hot water." She said, as if I cared.

"Sorry to hear that." I said.

She looked behind me and into my condo.

What the –?

I closed the door so only my face was visible.

"It's chilly out there today." I said.

"Are you having some kind of work done? Did you have the water shut off?" She persisted.

"No." I answered.

"Are you sure you're not having trouble?" She continued.

"Yes. I'm sure." I looked practically through her eyes, through her skull, and past the back of her head.

"Well, okay. I live on the other side of this condo on the opposite corner. If you have trouble just let me know." She said, still not smiling.

"Okay." I said and closed the door.

Like I'm really gonna' call you if I have a problem, lady.

I added this incident to my notes and tried to get some sleep.

The next day I came home from work, kicked off my shoes, and sat down to watch my show again.

Tap-tap-tap.

"O-M-G!" I said.

This time, I could tell it was coming from upstairs.

Are you kidding me? The neighbor is tapping?

I ignored the tapping and continued with my show and dinner. The neighbor tapped more and more until they got tired, I guess. Then the tapping stopped.

The next Monday, I was off from work. By some miracle, I got a little sleep that weekend. I woke up early to catch up on some work, but I got sleepy around 7:00 a.m. I was just about to go back to bed for a nap when I heard voices outside of my condo.

"No. I don't hear anything." A male voice said.

"How about now?" A lady said.

"Nope. Not now either." The man said.

"Well, I know something's going on." The lady said.

I headed to my bedroom when there was a knock on the door.

"Are you joking? At seven in the morning?" I said softly.

I looked through the peephole and saw a tall, muscular policeman. Out of curiosity alone, I had to open the door.

"Officer?" I asked.

"Yes. We received a complaint about some noise and some water and we had to come check it out." He said.

"My name is Jill Winston. My story is I am alone here. I work at Bay Diego Pier College. My security plan is that I don't talk to anyone and I keep to myself. I am not very big as you can see, so if someone wants to attack me, they will succeed. I am not very fast, so I can't outrun them. I try to be anonymous. You're welcome to come in if you want."

I stepped aside and he stepped into my condo.

"Noise and water? What's going on?" I asked.

"We received a complaint from the lady upstairs." He said. "Sorry to bother you."

"I wonder if this has to do with this weird note I received last week." I showed it to him. "It's anonymous. Someone left it on my door and it freaked me out"

He looked confused as he read it. "What?" He kept reading it until the end.

"Yeah, it's nutso." I said. "I don't have an electrical tool. I don't work at Solana Beach. I do not use my bathroom much because I don't like it. I want to replace the old sink and tub, so I have been showering at the gym. I also hate doing dishes so I eat takeout a lot and throw my takeout containers away. So, I don't know about the water."

The policeman looked into my room toward my bathroom and he looked in the direction of my kitchen.

"Well, the call has been checked on and there's nothing here. Sorry to bother you." He said.

"Just a minute. I have a 'Mrs. Kravitz' upstairs and I think this must be related to the note. I don't know how to fight back. I have done nothing wrong and it appears she has called the police on me." I said.

"You could go to the main office and ask there." He offered.

"There is no office on site. These are all independent condos." I informed him.

"Hmm." He thought.

"Well, I am going to have to be assertive with her because I don't want this to happen again." I said.

He was about to walk outside just as a little, elderly lady came down from upstairs and she walked right into my condo.

"You have to stand outside of the door." He told her.

She looked at me and said, "Oh, I didn't expect you here."

"You must have left me this note." I said.

"Yeah, but there was a man here before." She said.

"Well, I can guarantee you there is no man here now." I said. "It's just me and I am a woman."

"There used to be a man down here." She said. She looked around confused.

"Not anymore." I said. "I am a very nice person. All you had to do was come down here and introduce yourself to me, but you didn't do that. No, you went and called the State and I have done nothing wrong. If you had only come down here and introduced yourself, you would have known that I don't work at Solana Beach. I teach at the college over here." I pointed. "I don't sell insurance and I have no idea about any tool or any water."

The policeman walked outside of my condo. He stood nearby and watched us talk.

"Well, I didn't know." She said.

"No, you didn't, and what goes on down here is none of your business anyway." I told her.

"There was a guy down here and I heard some kind of tool." She said, confused.

"We're done here." The policeman said.

I shut the door.

I called Victoria.

"Vic'." I groaned

Yeah." She said.

"You will not believe what just happened." I told her.

"What now?" She asked.

"The cops just left here." I said.

"What? Never a dull moment!" She said.

"Some little, elderly lady left me that stupid note." I lamented.

"What? WTF?" She said.

"I know. I know. She needs to mind her own business. Had the cops all up in my place, too!" I said.

"That's crazy." She said.

"Isn't it, though?" I said.

"You writin' all this stuff down?" She asked.

"You know it." I said.

"Girl, you had finally found a perfect spot but then came all this drama." She said.

"I know. I know." I said.

"I want to come out there, but it's going to take me a while to get a flight and see if my mom can help Michael with the kids while I'm gone." She said.

I knew she was planning the trip in her head.

"So far, I'm okay. You know my house is always open to you, but don't kill yourself trying to get out here now." I said.

"Well, okay." She seemed reluctant to stop planning. Victoria was the world's greatest bestie.

I called my parents next.

"Mom. Dad." I said.

"Yes. We're both on." Mom said.

"Mom. Dad. The police were just here." I told them.

"The police? What?" My mom was surprised.

"Uh-huh. What happened, baby girl?" My dad asked.

"He said the lady upstairs called about noise and water. It turns out she is the one who left me that weird note." I told them. "He said he had to come check it out."

"Then what happened?" My dad asked.

"Well, he said he checked it out and there was nothing to report. He apologized. But then this elderly lady from upstairs came down the stairs and right into my condo. The cop made her stand outside. I set her straight." I said.

"Wow." My mom said.

"Then the cop said 'We're done here' before the lady could say more." I said.

"Well, that's good." My mom said. "It could have been worse."

"Are you still taking notes?" My dad asked.

"Oh, absolutely." I said.

"Good." He said. "Keep them handy just in case."

How does my dad always seem to know what to do and how to help me calm down?

A few weeks passed. No one tapped. For a few weeks I was able to eat dinner and watch my show. Nothing happened. . . until the next day.

Knock-knock-knock.

"Not again." I said softly.

I answered the door. By now my anonymity was dwindling so I had nothing to lose.

"Is this your mail?" Another brunette lady stared at me as she tried to see into my apartment. This time I kept the door near my face. She showed me a letter addressed to Rick Tartaliof.

"No!" I scoffed.

Lady, do I look like a Rick to you? And why didn't you just put this stupid envelope back into the mailbox?

"Yeah. I guess not." She tried to look past me into the condo again. I stared her down with a quizzical expression. She lingered for three seconds before she finally walked away.

I grabbed my file and added this latest incident. I reviewed my notes. Tapping, knocking, a stranger wondering about water, the police came by, a stranger wondering about mail.

Could this place get any weirder? Perhaps it was a mistake to move here.

I did some deep breathing exercises and started to get sleepy. I wanted to go to sleep and forget the day. I crawled into bed and sleep mercifully took over.

A few hours later, my chest hurt. I started coughing. I woke up.

Did I leave the kitchen gas on?

I had a lot of trouble breathing and the place smelled awful. Something was burning.

I coughed some more as I staggered toward the kitchen. The burners were all off. I tried to open the balcony door but the odor was stronger. I opened the front door but the smell was out there. Someone upstairs was smoking weed.

It had come down through their fireplace into mine. I tried to go into the bathroom, but the funk had wafted down there, too.

I looked upwards and yelled, "Why do I have to smell your funk at three in the morning?"

I heard hurried footsteps upstairs. I turned on the bathroom fan and every area fan in my condo. It helped slightly. At least I wasn't choking anymore, but I was extremely angry.

I tried to block everything out and go back to sleep.

The next day, I came home from work, kicked off my shoes, and turned on my show. I grabbed a bite to eat and then called Victoria.

"Hey." She said.

"Girl, you will not believe what happened." I said.

"What this time?" She said.

"I nearly choked to death last night." I said.

"What?" She said.

"Yeah. There's some pot smoker upstairs." I told her.

Suddenly I heard some screaming.

"What was that?" She asked.

"I'm not sure." I told her.

"I cannot believe that place." She said. "It's taking everything for me not to come out there for at least a weekend."

The screaming continued. I walked toward the noise. To my amazement, it seemed to be coming from the upstairs balcony.

"It's that nosy lady from upstairs." I told Victoria. "She seems to be screaming out into the night."

"That's crazy." She said.

"I know." I said. "I don't know what to do. I don't want to call the police. I've had about enough of them."

"Well, maybe if you wait her out, she will get tired." Victoria said.

"Yeah, maybe." I said.

We hung up and I continued with my dinner and my show. The screaming finally stopped and I went to sleep.

A few days later, I went to check my mail. I passed by another condo in the complex that was having an open house. I took the brochure to check the price and see what they'd done with the interior. It was beautiful. This unit was near the pool and the gym, too.

I'd love to buy this place. I could get away from the lady upstairs, have a bigger place, and be near the pool. That would be nice.

The asking price was a bit high, so I put it out of my mind. I got my mail and went back home.

The next morning, as I was about to leave for work, the piano playing started up again.

I stopped to listen. *Fewer sour notes. His practicing is paying off it seems.*

I grabbed my keys and headed out.

Ten days later, someone knocked on my door again.

This time I am going to tell them to just put the mail into the outgoing mailbox. That should be obvious.

I looked through the peephole. It was the police again, only this time there were two officers.

"Is everything okay?" I asked them.

"We received a call about some noise and some water." One officer said.

"Another officer was here not even two weeks ago asking the same thing." I said.

"We had that on record and that it was already addressed. It's a little confusing." The officer said.

"Do you need to come in?" I asked them.

"No. We were just checking on this call." The officer said.

I noticed that these officers were older. They had kind faces.

"My story is that my name is Jill Winston." I handed them my driver's license because I was ready this time. "I teach at the college over here." I pointed. "As my way of being safe, I keep to myself. I just go to work and come home. I am not a very big person and I'm not very fast so if someone wants to attack me, I'm as good as theirs. I do not talk to people here, but now, my anonymity is gone. I can see the folks in the building behind you looking down at us now from behind their curtains." I pointed up at them and a few pulled their faces away from the window. "I've even had strangers come by to give me mail they thought was mine. I don't like that at all and I don't know why they don't just give it back to the mail carrier."

The officers just listened intently. I was grateful for that.

"The lady upstairs has been making up stories about me and she left this anonymous note on my door." I showed it to them. "Getting that note was nerve-racking because, again, I keep to myself. I wondered who was watching me. I already told the other officer my story."

The officers read the note and handed it back to me.

Just then the piano practicing music started up again.

"Well, I don't hear any noise. I just hear the piano music." The officer said. "And I don't see any water that we should be concerned about."

"Something else has happened. In the last few days, I've heard the lady upstairs screaming into the night from her balcony. That's been quite weird."

"Uh-huh. It sounds like she might need care." He said.

Just then the second officer went back upstairs and the first officer stepped back and looked upstairs.

"Ma'am, we have checked on your complaint. There is no water and there is no noise. We need you to leave that nice lady downstairs alone now, okay?" He told her.

"But she has some electrical tool down there. I heard it." She said. "You should look for that."

"There is nothing down there that we are concerned about." The second officer told her.

"I am considering selling this place and moving out." I said.

The first officer turned back towards me and said, "We will look into whether there is someone who can look after the lady upstairs. Maybe she has some family we can call. Sorry to bother you twice. Have a good night."

"Same to you. Thank you, sir." I shut the door.

I've only been here a few months and I cannot believe what's happened. Do I want to sell this place?

I sat down and started considering my options. I liked the condo. It was near the beach and two freeways. There was great shopping and dining and it was fairly quick to get to the airport. I didn't want to leave, but with the problem lady upstairs, I didn't want to stay, either.

I was on my way out the door the next morning. I stopped to double lock the door when my neighbor on the quad motioned for me to come over. This was the first time she had spoken to me since I moved in. Perhaps she was like me, just keeping to herself for safety.

"My name is Zahira." She said.

"Jill. Nice to meet you, Zahira." I said.

She showed me a note. It had the same handwriting and the same stationery.

I have been having problems with the person downstairs. It's noisy and the TV is too loud. I am trying to deal with it. I called the police.

"I sometimes get notes from different people about my son's piano playing, but there's nothing that says he can't practice during regular waking hours. I just ignore them." She said.

"I've heard the playing. I know it's just practice, but it's actually nice. I have heard him improve over the last few weeks."

She smiled.

"I hope that when I am elderly, my neighbors will be compassionate toward me." I said.

"Yes. Well, I just wanted you to know." She said.

"Know what -- that she is talking to the neighbors about me now?" I said.

She shrugged. "I just ignore them."

"Thank you for the information. Again, it was nice to meet you. See you later." I said.

I headed to work seriously considering selling my condo. The situation wasn't just between the elderly lady and me, it was now spreading to my neighbors. I didn't like it.

That Friday after work, I went back to the beach. I breathed in the sea air.

Sure beats the funk of burnt skunk.

I looked up. There were my blue skies and miles of ocean waves. I sat back in my seat and relaxed.

Should I sell my condo?

I didn't want to. I had a great job. I was near the beach. I loved the location. I had a great life if you didn't count the drama. I had to admit that it was some pretty major drama. I decided to get away for the weekend. I booked a room at a beach hotel. I drove home to pack a bag for my weekend retreat.

There was Zahira in the parking garage.

"Hi, Jill." She said.

"Oh, hi, Zahira." I said.

She looked at my bags. "You're not leaving, are you?"

"Not just yet." I said.

Zahira went on. "I saw Irene. That's the elderly lady upstairs. She said she kept hearing things all day. I told her you were at work so no one was home. There was no way the noise came from you. She said she is concerned something might be wrong with her."

"I already know she hears things. You know the cops have been to my place twice already and not heard anything." I said.

"Yes." She said.

"Well, I'm going to grab a bite to eat. Thanks for the information." I said.

"See you later." She said.

I hopped in my car and headed to my retreat. I was determined to relax and enjoy myself.

I came back home Sunday afternoon. I saw an ambulance parked in front of the complex. I headed to my condo and saw people standing in my quad. The medics' heads were down. The police were there again, taking notes. I hoped this had nothing to do with me. There was Zahira. When she saw me coming, she walked over to me.

"Irene died." She said. "Her son came over for a visit and found her in the unit."

"Wow." I said. "That is sad news."

Depending on how you look at it. . .

I slapped my hands in my head. *Shame on me for thinking that.* But I didn't feel ashamed.

"He wants to sell the place quickly." She said.

"Oh." I said.

I went into my house to think. I waited until the police and medics left and the crowd thinned out. I looked outside and saw a man standing alone.

That must be the son.

I went outside and said, "Excuse me."

He turned around.

"I just heard about Irene. I am very sorry for your loss." I said.

"Thank you." He said.

"My name is Jill." I said.

"I'm Keith." He said.

"The neighbors said you were trying to sell your condo, Keith." I said.

"That's right. The sooner the better. I cannot make the payments. It's hard to deal with my mother's passing away and the bills and this place." He said. He seemed very tired as well as sad.

"I would like to buy the condo. Do you think we could discuss it after you've had a little time?" I asked.

"Yes. How about tomorrow at say 10:00 a.m.?" He asked.

"Yes. Ten's good." I said.

The next day we met inside of Irene's condo. It was a little creepy being inside of her place, but I pulled myself together because I wanted the condo.

Keith was packing up and clearing out. He had left a table and two chairs. He had the deed and other paperwork spread out on the table.

Wow. He really meant it when he said he wanted to sell quickly.

We signed all of the forms and I paid Keith for the condo. He gave me the deed, then cleared away the rest of Irene's belongings. The condo was mine.

I took time to savor the feeling of owning my second condo. It felt really, really good.

It didn't take long for me to find renters. Two students at my school had been looking for a place to rent. I rented it to them.

There was no tapping. No one came by to give me any mail. No one asked about my hot water. No one left odd notes on my door. The police never came by.

My cell phone rang.

"Hi, Vic'." I said.

"I am at the airport. Will you come and get me?" She asked.

"I'll do better than that. Let's go to Coronado Island. It's time to celebrate!" I said.

I picked up Victoria and we headed to Coronado Island. We went to a restaurant for dinner and sat outside at a beachfront table.

"So. What are we celebrating?" Victoria asked me.

"Well, Vic'," I sighed. "I took a lot of hits, but things got better in the end." I said.

"Do tell." She said.

"That lady, Irene, died." I told her.

"Really? Wow. After all the grief she caused, this is how it ended?" Victoria said.

"Yes. But there's more." I said.

"What?" She asked.

"I bought her condo and now I'm renting it out." I said.

31

"You were a real fighter, but you ended up on top. This was a long time coming." Victoria said. "Let's have a toast."

Victoria raised her glass. "To success!"

"To success!" We clinked glasses.

The sunset glistened on the ocean waves. I breathed in deeply just as I had on the first day. I took a sip. That was the sweetest wine I had ever tasted.

I love the taste of success.